Tiger and Me

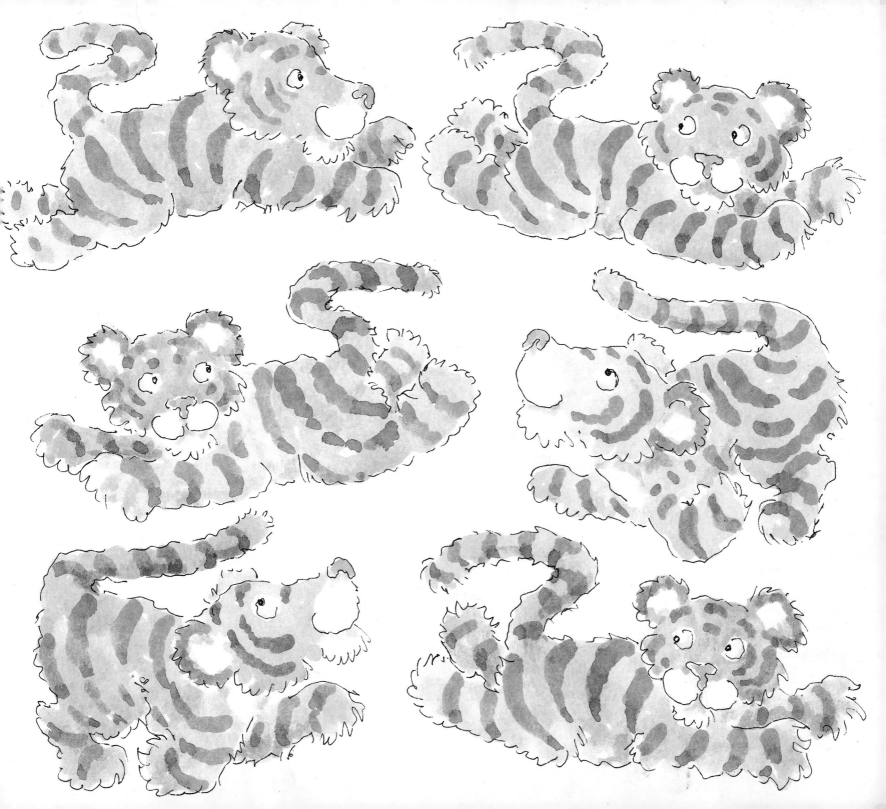

A Red Fox Book

Published by Random Century Children's Books
20 Vauxhall Bridge Road, London SW1V 2SA

A division of the Random Century Group
London Melbourne Sydney Auckland
Johannesburg and agencies throughout the world

First published by Hutchinson Children's Books 1990

Red Fox edition 1991

Text © Kaye Umansky 1990
Illustrations © Susie Jenkin-Pearce 1990

Printed and Bound in Hong Kong

ISBN 0 09 972210 0

Kaye Umansky

Tiger and Me

Illustrated by
Susie Jenkin-Pearce

RED FOX

I went to the jungle.
I met a small tiger.
I said to the tiger,
'Well, how do you do?'

The tiger said, 'Terrible.
Life is unbearable.
All of my brothers
Are locked in a zoo.

'No one to roar with me,
Roll on the floor with me,
No one to sing with me
Under the stars.

'No one to drink with me
Down at the water hole,
All of my brothers
Are locked behind bars.

'One week ago, we were
Peacefully sleeping,
Dreaming our dreams
Beneath tropical skies,

'When out from the shadows
The Zoo Men came creeping,
Moonlight reflecting
The whites of their eyes.

'I saw the hooks and
The snares and the blow pipes.
I saw the nets and
The ropes and the crate.

'Shouting a warning,
I raced for the undergrowth.
I got away, you see,
They were too late.

'Down came the net,
And my brothers were tangled.
Snarling and snapping,
How bravely they fought.

'But fangs are no use
Against Man's mighty weapons.
Soon it was over:
My brothers were caught.

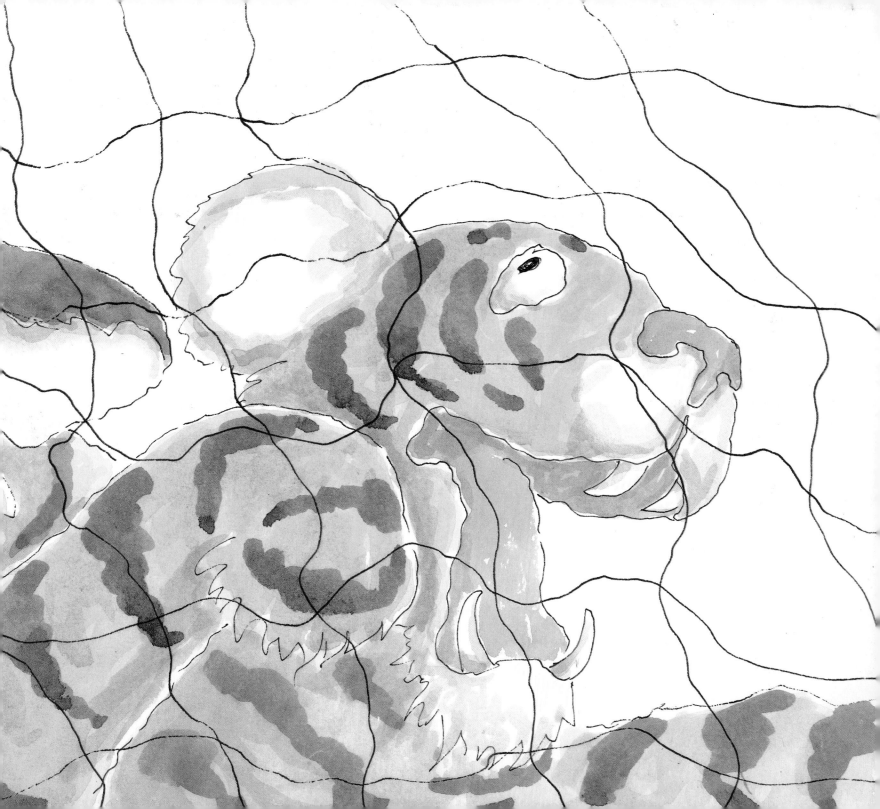

'Cages, for tigers,
Are places of misery.
Jungles are places
Where tigers should be.

'In this whole jungle
There's only one tiger.
One little tiger alone,
And that's me.'

I said to the tiger,
'Well tiger, that's terrible.
No one should be
Quite as lonely as you.

I'd like to help you
If you will allow me.
Leave it to me
I know just what to do.'

I left the tiger
And I left the jungle.
Hearing him talking
Had made me so sad.

I told his story
To those who would listen.
Mainly the children,
Of course, and my dad.

We wrote to the newspapers,
Phoned up the government,
Wrote a petition,
Complained to the zoos,

Saw the Prime Minister,
Organized marches –
And me and my dad,
We appeared on The News!

Wrongs can be righted
If you are determined.
We never gave up,
And we MADE them agree.

They took all the tigers
Back home to the jungle,
Opened the cages
And set them all free.

And that little tiger
I met when out walking?
Under the stars he is
Singing his song.

He and his brothers
Are frolicking joyfully
Down by the water hole,
Where they belong.

Other titles in the Red Fox picture book series (incorporating Beaver Books)